Indian Stories

Retold by Robert Hull
Illustrated by Noël Bateman
and Claire Robinson

Thomson Learning

New York

Tales From Around The World

African Stories
Caribbean Stories
Central and South American Stories
Egyptian Stories
Greek Stories
Indian Stories
Native North American Stories
Norse Stories
Roman Stories
Stories from the British Isles

Series editor: Katie Roden
Series designer: Tracy Gross
Book designer: Mark Whitchurch
Consultant: Dr. P. Mitter, Department of African
and Asian Studies, University of Sussex
Color artwork by Noël Bateman
Black and white artwork by Claire Robinson
Map on page 47 by Peter Bull

First published in the
United States in 1994 by
Thomson Learning
115 Fifth Avenue
New York, NY 10003

Published simultaneously in Great Britain in 1994 by
Wayland (Publishers) Ltd.

Library of Congress Cataloging in Publication Data

Hull, Robert.
  Indian Stories / retold by Robert Hull; illustrated by Nöel
Bateman.
      p.   cm.—(Tales from around the world)
  Includes bibliographical references.
  Summary: A collection of eight traditional tales from India
includes "The Buddha and Death," "Shiva Goes Fishing," and
"How Ganga Came Down to Earth."
  ISBN 1-56847-189-0
  1. Tales—India. [1. Folklore—India.] I. Bateman, Nöel, ill.
II. Title. III. Series.
PZ8.1.H883In   1994
398.2'0954—dc20   94-9718

Printed in Italy

Contents

Introduction

On the map, a huge "V" of land hangs down under the Himalayas, shaped like a fat bunch of grapes. The branch from which it hangs is a ring of huge mountains which cuts it off from the rest of the continent of Asia, though not totally; which is why this "V," India, is called a "subcontinent."

This subcontinent is like the largest and most colorful marketplace in the world. There are many Indias on display in India. There are a great number of languages to hear and at least ten different ways of writing them. There are different religions: Hinduism, Islam, Buddhism, Sikhism, Jainism, and Christianity, with their own beliefs, customs and stories. Even the word "India" means different things. It means, as well as the whole subcontinent, the separate country that shares the subcontinent with other countries: Pakistan, Bangladesh, Nepal, Sri Lanka, Bhutan.

But when we open a book of stories and read about holy men or elephants or monsters or demons or gods, we don't seem to notice these differences. And it doesn't seem to matter which part of India a story comes from; it's still Indian. Perhaps that is because the stories have been free to go where they wanted, like the wandering horse in the tale about Ganga, which was set loose to roam wherever it liked. Or like nomads, wandering people, such as the Indo-Aryans who came to India from southern Russia – bringing their stories – in about 1500 B.C.

Since all that time ago, storytellers have traveled throughout India. They didn't carry books, only amazing memories crammed with thousands and thousands of lines. They plied to and fro like containerships of the mind, with a cargo of tales. And people are still willing to sit up all night to hear about familiar moments in the life of Rama or in mischievous Krishna's boyhood, or to tales of the fights between gods and demons and of reincarnation, when the soul travels from one body to another, like a train stopping at the next station.

Some stories must have been told and told again for nearly 3,000 years. Thousands of stories still go here and there along India's paths and tracks, and in this book you can meet a few of them.

The Rain God and the Drought Demon

Of the earliest gods in India, three had the most power – Indra, Surya, and Agni. Indra was the god of rains and the sky, Surya was the sun god, and Agni was the god of fire. As well as gods, there were powerful demons, who fought the gods for control over "the three worlds": earth, the stars, and heaven. One of the most important battles was the struggle between Indra and Vritra, demon of drought and death.

Indra, the leader of the gods, was one of the makers of the world. His enormous strength pushed the sky up above the earth, and into that space he brought the dawn and the first sunlight. He sent atmosphere swirling through the gap, and clouds, and pulled down the first rains to refresh the earth. Next Indra cracked open mountains and struck fissures deep into the hills. Water sprang from the rocks, and streams tumbling down the mountains joined together to become great, rushing rivers.

Many demons resisted Indra. Every time he braced himself to pull open a mountain or clear a path for water or light, he felt their clinging power fighting against him. But few of them were strong enough to resist him, and one by one Indra broke their strength and destroyed them.

One enemy was a real danger. This was Tvashtri, who, like Indra, was a maker of things. Tvashtri was the craftsman who made water and fire. He designed the glittering palaces of the gods and made weapons for them, such as Indra's thunderbolt. He was even supposed to design husbands for wives before either of them was born.

Tvashtri was jealous of Indra, and always on the watch to harm him. Tvashtri saw his chance after the birth of his son. This son, Trishiras, whose mother was a demoness, grew three terrifying, mountain-sized heads. With one he read sacred books and practiced yoga, with another he ate and drank wine, and with the third he gazed around at the world. Trishiras became more and more powerful, and Indra began to fear him.

"Trishiras gazes around at the world with heads like three blazing suns," Indra said. "He is ready to drink up the sky. He wants to control the three worlds."

Feeling the mounting thought-energy of Trishiras, Indra became more and more concerned for his own power. So, attacking Trishiras with his lightning-blade, Indra cut off all his heads.

Tvashtri planned revenge for his murdered son. Bringing together all the white furies of his great mind, he focused them to create a super-demon to defeat Indra. When the demon was brought to life and finished it was called Vritra. Vritra had no hands or feet, and possessed the body of a sea-sized serpent with scales glittering like a million moons. He hissed and spoke: "Who am I? What am I for?"

"You are Vritra. I have brought you to life for a purpose."

"What am I here to do?"

"To kill Indra! To grow and grow and fill the space between earth and sky. To stifle the energy of earth and sky. Then Indra will die."

"That is many purposes," Vritra hissed. Then he writhed, and started to grow. In a few hours the demon had swollen to every horizon. He took up all the space and there was hardly any air. His heavy presence stifled the plains and oppressed the valleys. The outlines of mountains and peaks, which Indra had made clear and firm, seemed to sag and waver. The dusty glare of Vritra's long body lay across the mountains, burying the stars and imprisoning the dawn.

Everything that lived and moved in the narrow space between the shimmering earth and the sagging sky felt

the numbing power of Vritra. The monkeys were too tired to leap about in the trees or catch fish. Cows and bulls moved as if they were asleep. Elephants went slow-legged, as if they carried burdens of stone. Fetters of exhaustion hung on farmers in the fields.

Indra realized that Vritra had chained the rains. Rivers and streams felt their power leave them as they flowed slower and slower, then not at all. After that the demon drank all the springs and wells and filled them with dust. Little imps of dust scurried under the trees and across the fields.

After a time there seemed to be nothing but Vritra. His immense shape swayed and dazzled in front of people's eyes. The trees died and crops turned to dust. The bleached bones of animals lay everywhere.

During the time of Vritra there was not one drop of rain. Though dark clouds sometimes marched through the narrow pass between earth and sky, none of them would release any of their waters. Indra threw some thunder and lightning, but they were too weak to split the clouds open.

Vritra had swallowed up the world. He had stolen the earth and the air. He had taken all the water and the clear sky was covered over by his fierce, dusty glare. He had deprived creatures of the power to move.

It seemed as if he had killed Indra. There was no sign of the great god of rains and the air. He was lost, swallowed up, his strength and power nowhere to be seen.

But still everyone prayed to Indra, begging him to return and defeat the demon. The hymns and prayers slowly gave him energy. He reached into the atmosphere and clenched it in his fists till lightning sparked. He found his colored bow hanging in front of the weakened thunder of the last waterfall, and fired a shower of glistening arrows into the dark cloud-towers that swirled around Vritra. His thunder-blade went curving and crackling under the low sky.

It was not enough. Though he squeezed the dark clouds till they growled and muttered, they refused to part with their rain. Try as he could, Indra could not defeat Vritra without help. He went to Vishnu to ask for advice.

"Go to Vritra. Take sages and wise gods," said Vishnu. "Talk peace with him. You will find a way of getting rid of him. And when the time comes, I will lend my strength to the power of your thunderbolt."

So Indra went with many sages and minor gods to Vritra. A sage spoke first: "Vritra, the whole world is in your power. But Indra, just as strong with life and energy, fights against you. In the struggle, creatures are dying, men and women, animals and birds. Instead of war between you, let there be peace."

Vritra replied, "If enemies fight all the time and harm the earth, there is no rest for the world. I will agree to a truce, but Indra must swear never to kill me by night or day, not with any weapon of metal or stone or wood, not with anything dry or wet. If Indra agrees to this for all time, I will agree."

Indra nodded his head slowly.

And so it was agreed that Indra and Vritra should not fight for absolute power. Each would have to let the other live. Sometimes Indra with his rains would rule, sometimes Vritra with his drought.

10

But Indra was not satisfied. He still looked for a way to be rid of the threat of Vritra. One day he saw the demon at sunset at the edge of the sea. "I could kill him now, at sunset," thought Indra. "It is not night, and it is not day."

At the same moment he saw something that was not metal, or stone, or wood, that was not wet or dry. A mass of foam had been blown across the beach into a great pile like a small mountain. In it were some dead birds and fish, choked by lack of air.

Indra remembered that Vishnu had promised to help him, and began to drive the foam towards the serpent Vritra. Suddenly he felt Vishnu's power flood into his own, whipping up his breath to the force of a typhoon as it hurled mud and foam up at the demon.

The huge body of Vritra, choking, began to fall back towards the earth. The top of the sky shone clear again. Vritra's broken form reeled back from the clouds like a million ropes of dark haze falling. The gap between sky and earth opened wide again, and the clear atmosphere swirled back through the gap, like a tide flowing over the beach.

At last the rains came sweeping over the dry land. A thousand pools appeared from nowhere. The forests steamed with wetness. The mountains shone silver as streams spilled down their sides.

The demon of drought and famine never recovered his old strength. From that time Indra was always the stronger of the two.

A Glimpse of the Future

*I*t was an ordinary village morning. Birds sang, men gossiped. The farm animals went wandering around making farm animal noises, or just lay in the dust. Dogs sniffed each other. It was peaceful and sunny. Under a banyan tree an aged guru was talking to his pupils about the next life.

"Now, in the next body, which you will all enter, whether it be a human body or a monkey's, or a dog's, or a chicken's, or an ant's, or…" Suddenly he stopped in the middle of his sentence.

His young audience saw a look of puzzlement spread over their teacher's face. They saw it turn slowly to horror. His eyes had focused on the ground near his feet. He seemed to be staring at something there in the dust.

"Please, leave me for a while, leave me," he said, his voice shaking. "Come back to me in the evening."

The students scrambled up and left their guru to his thoughts. Later that day, as the sun dropped in the sky, they returned to the banyan tree, puzzled about what he might say to them.

"My young pupils, this morning, while I spoke to you of the bodies of ants and chickens and monkeys and humans, I had a vision of the future. I saw what I am destined to become in the next life. I even had a glimpse of myself, already living my next life."

The pupils turned to each other, whispering and smiling about how such a holy guru was certain to become a splendid saint or a noble king, perhaps even a minor kind of god. The guru interrupted them: "I want one of you, in return for the wisdom I have given you, to help me with a task I have in mind."

All the pupils crowded forward, saying, "Master, master, let me be the one." The guru held up his hand. "It is a difficult, unpleasant task. When I tell you what it is, you will wish to avoid it."

But the pupils still said they would do whatever he asked. So they settled the question of who it would be by choosing lengths of straw from his hand. A very young student drew out the shortest straw. He was to perform the guru's task. He started thinking what it could be. "My teacher, tell me what I have to do, so that I can immediately start to enjoy thinking about it."

"This morning, while I was speaking, I learned that I was to be reborn very soon. I also learned what, after an interval of time, I was to be reborn as."

The students looked at each other in dismay. Their guru to leave them soon! Perhaps he was to become a god? A king? A lion? A large tortoise? They did not dare guess, for fear of causing offense. The guru continued.

"I am to become…" he paused. "I am to return as…You observe that sow over there, the immense one snuffling up garbage and peelings? Well, in a short while I am destined to reappear on earth as a pig. Yes, a pig. To be precise, as the fourth piglet in that hulking sow's next litter. And my reincarnation will occur fairly soon, by the look of her."

The young disciples could not believe their ears. Their guru to be reborn as a piglet! To fall from meditation to mud, from purity to piggery in one tragic tumble!

The guru went on to give instructions to the chosen student. "You will recognize me. As fourth piglet, I shall have a mark on my brow. After a day or two I want you to take your knife, find the marked piglet and slaughter it. That way you will release my soul from its prison of pig, and send me quickly to my next life."

The student was horrified at the idea of his guru becoming a pig, but just as horrified at the idea of murdering him. Though it would only be a pig, the pig

13

would be his ex-teacher. But he had promised. Later that week the guru died, and the day after that the sow had four piglets.

A few days later the young student took his knife to slaughter the guru-piglet. He came upon the whole litter slumped on their sides in the sun after a good feed. Their fat stomachs were going up and down like seesaws and they were all snoring in a whistling enjoyable way like a band of small, fat, pink musicians. It seemed a pity to disturb them, but the student found his ex-teacher, with the mark on his forehead, lying tucked deep in the sow's side. He bent to pick him up. As one hand grasped the skin at the back of the piglet's neck and the other tightened on the knife, the piglet woke.

In a flash the piglet saw what was happening. He also vaguely remembered asking someone to do something for him, someone in some other distant, uninteresting life. Yes, to slaughter him! That was all very well for a guru in another life to ask, but this piglet was no longer that guru. What is more, he had just woken from a very pleasant dream, in which he'd been lying in cool mud listening to the birds after a good slop around in the swill and muck. He had been on earth a few days and knew what its pleasures were.

All this flashed through the young pig's brain as he saw the glint of a knife raised above him. Even without being told, a piglet knows what a knife is, and he squealed. It was a terrorized scream of a squeal, like a hundred cart axles grating at once.

"No, no, don't kill me! Let me live! Let me go on being a pig! A pig's life is wonderful! The muddiness and the slushiness, the scraps and the swill, our mother's great, snoring, hot body, our cute, curly tails – everything is too good to stop. I want to go on being this me-pig for as long as possible and then come back as another one, even if it has to be in a different farmyard with different garbage and birds and humans."

The student didn't know what to do. But he put his knife down and went back to tell the others that he'd broken the solemn promise he made to his teacher before he died. It made him sad. Then he thought of how he'd given his old guru the chance of a good pig's life. That made him happy, but puzzled.

He didn't know what to think. "This life is very confusing," he said to himself. "Perhaps my next one will be simpler."

15

How Ganga Came Down to Earth

The Ganges is one of the great rivers of India. It is a sacred river, and the life of much of India depends on its precious waters. It flows south from the highest mountains in the world, the Himalayas, then eastward across the huge plain of Hindustan. Finally it enters the Indian Ocean near Calcutta. Nowadays, the Ganges is usually a serene and peaceful river, but long ago…

A powerful king called Sagara was making ready for the Horse Ceremony. In this ceremony, a horse was set loose to roam free across India. Wherever the horse went, whatever mountains, valleys, rivers, and fields it crossed would become the new lands of the king Sagara. It was Sagara's way of making his large kingdom even larger. The horse was followed by fierce warriors on horseback.

Neighboring kings had to accept Sagara's claim to increase his power in this way, or go to war against him. If anyone refused to let the horse pass, it was taken as a challenge and fighting would begin.

Sagara's kingdom had become an empire so powerful that Indra, leader of the gods, became nervous. He decided to prevent it from growing any bigger. The best way of doing this would be to intervene in the Horse Ceremony.

Indra disguised himself as a demon, and stole Sagara's horse. He led it down through a deep gorge into the underworld, and left it grazing there, in a secluded valley. The only inhabitant of the valley was a famous wise man, Kapila, who had chosen the place for his meditations.

When Sagara was told that his horse had disappeared, he spoke furiously to his many sons: "Find the thief! Scour the earth! Valley by valley, village by village! Look in every cave and hollow, on every hillside and at every river's edge. If my horse is not above the earth, look beneath it!"

The brothers went back and forth over the surface of the land for many years, but they could not find Sagara's horse. It must be hidden under the earth, they decided. But then they could not find the entrance to the underworld, so with their great hands, hard as metal from years of riding, they started to claw up the land and turn over the earth. Down and down their hands shoveled, throwing up half the whole earth in mountains of waste and spoil. Millions of trees, plants, creatures, and spirits died.

At last they broke into the underworld valley. Kapila was engaged in his meditations, and there, grazing quietly, was the horse.

"We have found him! Thief! Thief!" they cried. Taking rocks in their fists and hauling up trees by the roots, they went over to threaten Kapila.

But Kapila had enough power to confront them. Whether, as some people say, he was the son of Agni, the fire god, or whether Krishna himself had taken the shape of Kapila to protect the earth, no one knows. But the ground split, and there was a dreadful roar as a river of flame bounded out and swirled over all but one of the sons of Sagara, burning them to ashes.

The one survivor, who had been hanging back in shame, fled home and told his father the grim story. Sagara, in despair, gave up his throne and made one of his grandsons king.

Many years later, Bhagiratha, the son of this new king, heard the story of the brothers burned to ashes by an outbreak of divine fire. The story horrified him and would not leave his mind.

"The ashes of my ancestors!" he said to himself, "In a gloomy valley beneath the earth, unburied, and unpurified by the touch of water! Their sad spirits hang in the empty air, trapped and motionless."

Bhagiratha knew it was his mission to free his ancestors. Common offerings of water would not be pure enough for the ashes of those burned by the anger of the gods, so he journeyed to the forests of the Himalayas to meditate alone. There, for many years, he prayed to Brahma, the creator, for help.

Brahma told him to ask the god Shiva to bring down the waters of Ganga, daughter of Himavan the mountain god – "the owner of the snow."

"Only water flowing through the white mountains of heaven," Brahma said, "will be pure enough for such a great task."

Bhagiratha prayed to Shiva for many more years. At the end of that time Shiva appeared and said, "I will try to persuade Ganga to come to earth. You must pray to her as well." Shiva gave Bhagiratha a horn. "If she does come you will need this to guide her."

And now Bhagiratha prayed to Ganga herself. Finally she appeared to him as a young girl and warned him of a danger: "If Ganga plunges foaming from the mountains of heaven straight down to earth, the land will be shaken and flooded and washed away. Earth cannot withstand the full might of Ganga. Say this to Shiva."

Ganga wished to keep her waters in heaven, not share them with earth. Even more, she wanted to oppose the wish of Shiva. This was because once, long ago, she had found herself in his terrible power. The gods had begged Shiva to sing his great song, the song that could move the earth and make the stars sway and dance. When Shiva sang the sea would rise up in a flood, wanting to reach up toward the heavens and join in the dance. Vishnu, protector of the world, had to sit in front of Shiva, like a rock before waves, to shield the earth from the wild, destructive strength of the song. But Ganga, hearing the song spread, flooding the world, had not been able to prevent herself rising under its power. She had spread among the mountains of heaven until she had nearly flooded them. It was Vishnu who prevented it, imprisoning the waters of Ganga in great rivers of ice.

Bhagiratha told Shiva what Ganga had said about earth not being able to withstand her full might. But Shiva had already decided that Ganga should descend. Bhagiratha had spent many years in prayer and meditation, and had earned his reward.

Ganga could not finally resist Shiva's will, but she thought her bodily strength could defeat him. Believing that the power of her falling waters could wash him away, she hurled herself outward from the immense mountain-heights of heaven. She fell and fell for many years, twisting among the cloudy pinnacles of the sky, downward toward the waiting earth.

Shiva was also waiting. Where the shining waters of Ganga fell, he thrust his arms up among them. Ganga's foaming waters roared down on to his head, but instead of washing him away, the waters disappeared among the long, matted locks of the mountain god.

The waters of Ganga wandered for many years through the dense hair on Shiva's mountainous head, winding uncertainly here and there in a maze of different channels. When the waters finally emerged they spilled over the shoulders of the mountain god in seven shining streams.

Even after so long finding their way through Shiva's matted hair, the waters still had some of their thunder left. They dazzled the eye as they fell from his hair and wound across the dry earth, each stream searching for the right course.

Many of the lesser gods of earth came to look at the amazing sight, their jewels adding to the glitter and dance of light. Pale water nymphs and green forest demons came, and priests, singers, and musicians. All of them hurried to touch the pure waters of Ganga.

Bhagiratha had succeeded. His long waiting had brought sacred water to the earth. Now he had to guide it to the ashes of his ancestors. He blew a long note on the horn that Shiva had given him, and started out towards the deep gorge where the ashes lay.

The widest stream of Ganga followed the sound. It finally came to the entrance to the dark gorge and plunged steeply down, running to the ashes and swirling over them.

20

At that moment the spirits of the sons of Sagara were released, and crowded upward toward heaven. The great river ran on, until it came to the stupendous clefts and craters which the sons of Sagara had dug with their hands in their mad search for their father's horse. The waters of Ganga filled them all, and became the seas of the earth.

Ganga, wandering by a thousand villages, had brought life with her. The lotus bloomed. The water teemed with shoals of fish. The air shone with leaping porpoises. Herons came to inspect the river's edge and crocodiles elbowed their way over rocks to bask in the sun. Tortoises and crabs swam and clambered, and armies of brilliant water birds patrolled the mud.

Brahma spoke to Bhagiratha as he stood at the side of the river: "Bathe in these sacred waters, because they brought life back from the burnt ashes of life. Let Ganga be called your daughter, whom you brought down from heaven by ages of faith and prayer. Let these waters be called Ganges."

Ever since, Ganges has brought life to the burned plains. And thousands of small channels, as many as the years that Bhagiratha waited, glide off toward hazy distant hills, taking her precious waters to the fields where life begins again each year.

The people along those banks remember the story of Ganga's coming, especially when the moon rests its silver head on the water.

The Buddha
and Death

Siddhartha Gautama, who was called the Buddha, or "The Enlightened One," was born as a prince in about 563 B.C. Later he became a great holy man and teacher, and legends grew up around his life. One said that on his first day on earth he could walk, and that lotus flowers grew where he stepped. In other stories, like this one, some true history might be part of the legend.

A prophecy was made about the young prince Siddhartha. If he learned about sickness, old age and death, he would become a great saint instead of a great ruler. His father, who wanted Siddhartha to be king after him, decided to protect him from any knowledge of misery or age. He built a palace with three walls and three moats. There Siddhartha was surrounded, night and day, by nothing but pleasure and beauty.

Life slid by luxuriously in the pleasure gardens of the palace. Water from a hundred fountains fell into pools where young men and women swam and played among shoals of many-colored fish. Reflections of small bridges and elegant white buildings swayed and shimmered. Under the trees were high swings where couples went lazily to and fro. In sandy arenas, splendid horses hurtled around with their skillful riders. Stairs wound up to high terraces where people danced to stringed instruments and soft drums.

For Siddhartha there were always friends to spend time with, music to listen to, games to join in and tame creatures to play with. Nothing unpleasant was visible to him, and the very words "death," "age," and "misery" were forbidden.

Siddhartha Gautama was more than twenty years old when he left the palace for the first time. His father took him to a town for the games tournament being held there. He had decided that, as future ruler, Siddhartha had to take part. Still concerned about the prophecy, the king went to great lengths to see that the town was swept clean and filled with flowers. Sick beggars were taken away, and old people were told to keep off the streets.

But the preparations were not quite thorough enough. Siddhartha saw a shape he could not understand. It was the bent figure of an old man. Siddhartha had never seen a bent human figure, nor an old face. This shape shuffling along over a stick was not something he could make sense of. Then the old man fell, and lay still. Siddhartha's servant, Chandaka, ran over to where he lay.

"Why did he do that?" Siddhartha asked.

"He has collapsed," Chandaka replied, his head already listening for the man's heart.

Siddhartha questioned like a child: "Why? Is it a game?"

"He is very old, and he has died," was the reply.

"What is old? Has he always been old?"

"No, he was once young like you. He became old and has now died."

"Does it happen to many men?"

"It happens to all men and all women."

"Shall I be old? Must I die?"

"Of course."

Siddhartha was thoughtful and silent. He had never heard about old age or death. He returned home a changed man.

After that, the more he discovered about the death that ends life, the more he knew that he had to leave the protected world of the palace and travel outside its three walls. He had to know what the world was really like, and understand it.

This was how it came about that at the age of twenty-nine, leaving his wife and young son, Siddhartha Gautama set out to find wisdom. So the prophecy came true: Siddhartha had learned the meaning of death and would be a great saint, not a great ruler.

24

Nala and Damayanti

Nala, king of Nishadha, was famous for his skill as a sportsman and hunter and his knowledge as a scholar, and just as well known for great honesty. He was very handsome, too, and unmarried.

One day, walking in the palace garden, he saw a flight of wild swans settle on the lake. He watched them for a while and then, in a moment of hunter's zeal, he grasped the neck of one as it drifted at the water's edge among the lotus blooms. As the great bird thrashed its wings to escape, a voice from its beak hissed at Nala: "Let me go, let me go! I will fly to Vidarbha and praise you to Damayanti, the most beautiful woman in all India."

Nala stood transfixed. But birds and animals sometimes spoke, and Nala knew that the swan was sacred to the goddess of learning.

"Go then," said Nala. "A chance to meet the most beautiful woman in India is better than any meal of swan's flesh."

Nala let go of the bird's throat. The swan beat its way along the surface of the water and took to the air. The others followed in a din of wings.

Damayanti, daughter of king Bhima, lived in the neighboring kingdom of Vidarbha. The next day, swimming in a pool in the royal gardens, she heard the flutter of wings and the splashes as the swans came down near her. One paddled across to her and spoke, amazing her as it had amazed Nala.

"You are the loveliest woman in India. We have come from Nala, king of Nishadha. He is the most handsome and talented man in the world. He is the one you should marry."

Damayanti had never thought of marrying, but for the rest of the day she thought of nothing else. Before sunset she had begun to believe she could marry only Nala, whom she had never met. The next day she spoke her mind to the swan: "More than anything in the world I wish to see this Nala. Tell him that I have already begun to wait for him."

In the days after the swans had gone, Damayanti began to despair. She could see no way to meet Nala. She thought of him night and day. She ate less and less and grew thin.

It so happened that Bhima, Damayanti's father, was at this time planning a swayamvara, a feast for his daughter to which he would invite all the men who might want to marry her. Damayanti would choose who she wanted to marry from among the men who came.

"He must come to the swayamvara, he must come," Damayanti said to herself. If she could choose Nala for her husband her grief would be at an end.

Even as she talked desperately to herself, an official of Bhima's court, riding an elephant and beating a drum, was traveling through central India announcing the swayamvara. He visited Nishadha, and Nala was soon riding his favorite horse towards Vidarbha.

But the same news also arrived in heaven, at the houses of the gods. Indra, their leader, had become curious when he noticed that the kings of earth were not visiting him. When he asked why, he was told that they were going to a swayamvara for the most beautiful woman in India. Then and there, four of the chief gods decided to go as well. And down they plunged to earth, to the road near Vidarbha – Indra, god of skies and rain, Agni, god of fire, Yama, god of death, and Varuna, god of the oceans. A demon called Kali later heard about it as well, and he set out too, with a demon accomplice.

As it happened, the gods met Nala on the same road. "Here's a fine-looking fellow," said Indra. "He can take a message for us. Young man, off you go to Damayanti and tell her that we four gods intend to arrive and take part in the swayamvara. And point out to her that though there may be rich human kings present, a woman ought to marry a god whenever one becomes available."

Nala was appalled. "I have to compete with gods for Damayanti!" he thought wildly. "I even have to carry their messages!" But he could not refuse.

He had no need to carry their words far or for long. The gods flew him magically over the walls of Bhima's palace, into the garden where Damayanti was playing with the young women who attended her. He stumbled out of the sunlight under a banyan tree and saw the most beautiful woman he had ever seen. Damayanti turned and saw him. She and Nala gazed at each other. "It must be him," she thought. And Nala thought to himself, "I long to use words of admiration and love to Damayanti, and instead I have to speak this dreadful message."

"I am Nala. I have to give you these words from four gods. They are coming to your swayamvara. They say you must choose one of them." Then Nala told Damayanti the story of his meeting with them.

"Nala, I have never seen you until this moment, but I have waited for you and dreamed about you. No god will take me from you now. Tell them that."

Nala was overjoyed, but anxious as well. "Damayanti, can you choose a mortal man if the gods want you? And imagine the joys of sharing a god's life! It might mean death to refuse them."

"No, Nala, I have decided. You and the gods will come to the swayamvara, and I will choose you, and the gods can watch. They will have a good tale to tell in heaven."

Nala wondered whether he dare report what she said to the gods. Suddenly he found himself standing on the road with them. "I gave the message honestly," he said, "but Damayanti's reply" – Nala paused and looked around at them nervously – "her reply is that she will choose Nala – choose me, that is."

He had told them honestly what Damayanti had said. The gods laughed.

Through the city gates on the day of the swayamvara wound a river of color. Thousands of people pressed forwards toward the palace. Red, yellow, and blue chariots and carts creaked along. Animals carried emperors and kings and even musicians with instruments. Camels gazed around snootily. Elephants with banners and flags, and gold plates across their foreheads, splashed in tanks and pools to bathe and to drink.

What a din there was, with the noise of all the creatures and the cries of grooms, servants, and soldiers, and what brilliance in the glitter of pearls and gems on the clothes of the suitors and the jeweled harnesses of their mounts. Lucky people even found pieces of jewelry lying in the dust.

The moment came when Damayanti had to choose her husband. Her women-servants carried her slowly along in a swaying white palanquin, past rows and rows of handsome young men – and some not so handsome, or young either. They all looked up at her, smiling anxiously, not knowing that for all their good looks and jewel chests she wasn't considering them.

Then she saw Nala. But at the same moment she saw…another Nala! And another! And two more! Like the same reflection in five mirrors, she saw five Nalas.

"The cunning gods!" she thought at once. "They have taken Nala's shape so as to have the same chance as he! Which one is Nala? How can I choose him if I can't recognize him?" Damayanti stood gazing at all five figures, with tears in her eyes. She tried to remember all the signs by which you are supposed to be able to recognize gods, but all five Nalas looked just the same.

Then she had an inspiration. She said, "Noble gods, if you remember my sincere reply to your message, when I said I would still choose Nala, be sincere yourselves. Think of my despair. Do not play this cruel game with my feelings; show me who you really are, just as I showed you the sort of woman I was."

The gods were moved by her words, and suddenly Damayanti could see which four of the five figures were gods. Gods could either completely change into human form, or just imitate it. At first they were fully human;

28

now, hearing Damayanti's words, they became gods again, with only an appearance of being human. Four of the five Nala look-alikes now had no sweat on their brows. They had no dust on their feet, and they threw no shadows as they floated just above the ground.

As soon as Damayanti saw the Nala with a shadow, the real Nala with sweat glistening on his forehead, she said, "You, you are he. I choose you." And reaching down from the palanquin she hung a garland of flowers around his neck.

Nala trembled with joy. Shrieks of excitement went up from Damayanti's friends and women-servants, and groans of dismay from the ranks of suitors. But, thought Nala, what would the gods do?

Indra spoke: "The gods do not always win their battles. Nala, you have beaten us. Your honesty and Damayanti's courage are strong weapons."

The wedding feast was held, then off everyone went. Nala and Damayanti set out joyfully for their home in Nishadha, the emperors and kings rode gloomily toward their own countries, while the gods took the quiet road to heaven.

And there the story of Nala and Damayanti might have ended happily ever after, if it had not been for that certain demon named Kali. He finally set out for the swayamvara with his demon friend Dvapara, only to meet the gods climbing to heaven on their way back. They stopped. "And where are you off to, Kali?" Indra asked.

"To the swayamvara, of course. Why are you heading home?"

Laughing, they told him why he was too late. Kali was furious. As a demon, a being with godlike power, he couldn't believe that a man had been preferred to a god. "They will not survive. I will destroy them."

"It will be very difficult for you," Indra said. "You will find no chink of weakness there. Nala is a king among men. You will have to wait years before you see him being unkind, or untruthful, or unjust."

The gods tried to persuade him not to, but Kali decided to follow Nala and Damayanti to Nishadha. He would watch them, and wait for a hundred years if he needed to.

And so, as an invisible spirit, Kali began to haunt the court at Nishadha, waiting for an opportunity to strike, a moment of weakness or sinfulness. In the meantime Kali told Dvapara to enter into some dice; the evil he planned would lie there like a seed waiting for water.

Kali waited twelve years, while Nala and Damayanti lived happily and had two children. Then the demon's chance came. One day Nala simply forgot a part of his daily ritual; he went to prayers without first washing his feet.

It was enough. Kali slipped into the flaw like light through a crack in a box. Working in Nala's mind, he made Nala challenge his brother Pushkara to a game of dice. Pushkara was a very jealous brother. He had many reasons: Nala was king, and had Damayanti, and was more talented, wise, and kind than Pushkara. A game of dice was a perfect opportunity for Pushkara to show his brother up.

The dice already carried Dvapara's evil load. As they rolled, Dvapara swayed this way and that, tipping the dice over so that Pushkara won game after game. At first Nala lost only jewels and animals, then villages, estates, and even palaces were handed over. For many months the gambling went on and on, till there was hardly any money left in the treasury. The government was neglected, the officials unpaid.

"My luck will soon turn," Nala said whenever Damayanti implored him to stop. Finally she arranged for their two children to be taken back to her old home in Vidarbha and cared for there. By then Nala had only two things left that he could call his own – his kingship and his wife.

"Let us have one final game," Pushkara said. "If you win, you can have everything back. If I win, I take the country and the throne from you." The final, fatal game was played, and Nala's cold, contriving brother became king of Nishadha.

He immediately sent messengers around the country with a proclamation: "The ex-king Nala, the reckless gambler, has been ordered to leave the country. No citizen is allowed to feed, clothe, or shelter him, or to help him in any way. The penalty for disobedience is death."

"Damayanti has nowhere to go," Pushkara muttered to himself, "I have won her too."

Nala also thought so. He spoke to Damayanti: "I am only an imitation Nala. I have diced away my true self, and thrown away my claim to your love. Stay here with Pushkara. Perhaps there will be some happiness for you. There will be none with me." Without waiting for Damayanti's reply, and blinded by tears, Nala set out. He had hardly any food and only a single piece of cotton cloth to cover him.

But Damayanti, taking only the clothes she wore, soon followed him. She could not bear to be separated from Nala, or think of him in the forests alone. Soon she caught up with him, as he was trying to catch some golden-winged birds pecking on the ground. He managed to throw his single garment over them, but then they flew up into the

air, trailing the cotton cloth beneath them and shrieking, "We are Kali's birds, birds of the dice-spirits! Now you have nothing!"

That night Nala tried to persuade Damayanti to leave him. "I have nothing, not even clothing. With me you have no hope and you will starve. Go back to my brother, please."

"How can I leave? I could never go to Pushkara. There is hope as long as we're together. Tomorrow we will find clothing for you. Once we get to Vidarbha my father will help."

And so they wandered on. In a while they found a small forester's hut and, covered by Damayanti's dress, went to sleep. But Kali, who had never left Nala's mind, woke him up. In Nala's mind Kali placed the thought that even if Damayanti would not leave him, he ought to leave her. They would never get to Vidarbha; she could

return to Nishadha.

Even after he had made up his mind – or Kali had made up his mind for him – Nala could hardly tear himself away. But as Kali gazed at Damayanti's sleeping face, he summoned his utmost strength and twisted into shape one last thought for Nala. Nala took Damayanti's garment, tore it in two, and covering Damayanti with one piece, left wearing the other.

When Damayanti woke, the hut was lifeless. Nala had gone. She cried out at the empty hut: "Why have you left me, weak-headed husband? Did you not believe me?" But she had no thought of going back to Nishadha and Pushkara. She set out again after Nala, running and stumbling, on and on through the forest. Finally, worn out and looking older, she arrived at the city of King Subahu. When she fainted at the gates of the palace, her plight came to the attention of the queen, who had her brought inside.

Damayanti's story moved the queen to tears. She was given a few rooms of her own to live in as she waited for news of Nala.

In the meantime, Nala was having his own adventures. A short while after leaving Damayanti he came into a clearing where smoke rose from a circle of fire. He heard a voice calling, and in the middle of the flames he saw the human face and beautiful, glistening coils of a royal serpent, a naga. "Nala, I am cursed and circled by fire. Narada, Krishna's friend, has done this. Carry me ten paces out of the flames and you will have the thing you most long for."

Nala obeyed the royal creature, but while carrying it out of the flaming circle he felt a burning sensation in his hand. Reeling back, he threw down the snake. "I have been bitten! Poison in return for kindness!"

"My poison is already working to make a disguise for you and to preserve you. Your enemies will not know who you are until you are ready for them to know."

Nala looked down at his legs and felt his face. If he had had a mirror, he would not have known himself. The naga's poison had turned him into a bent-legged old man.

The naga slid near him and lifted his head to speak. "Listen. From now on, call yourself Vahuka the charioteer. Go to Ayodhya, to king Rituparna. Ask to work in his stables. The time will come – listen carefully – when you can exchange your skill at driving horses for Rituparna's skill with dice. When you want to return to your true appearance, wear this." And the naga handed to Nala a simple white cloak.

With that the regal naga slid away to his glittering palace under the earth.

Nala journeyed for days till he came to Ayodhya. There, as the naga had said, he became Vahuka the charioteer.

Both Nala and Damayanti had disappeared from the world. Many a group of messengers had gone from Damayanti's father, Bhima, to look for her. Finally, one came to the kingdom of Subahu and discovered their king's lost daughter. Overjoyed, she went home to Vidarbha.

Once she was at home, Damayanti chose messengers who had known Nala and would recognize him, and sent them out to search for him. They were to ask the question, "Where are you, king and gambler, who took half of his wife's only dress? Why don't you come home?"

After riding all over central India the messengers finally came to Ayodhya. When they read out their message, Nala-Vahuka, the old charioteer, trembled at the words "king…gambler…half of his wife's dress." The words told him that his wife was still alive and wanted to know about him. She might even have forgiven him. The messengers did not recognize him, but he managed to send a sort of reply to her. He sat near one of the messengers and said to him in a low voice, "He left her in the depths of the forest. She was abandoned, but her rage must have been calmed by love."

Nala had guessed that the messengers would report this strange little speech to Damayanti, and they did. "What did the man look like?" Damayanti immediately asked.

"Oh, he was old and bent-legged," she was told.

Damayanti was in agonies of uncertainty. "The words must somehow have come from Nala," Damayanti thought, "but the speaker of the words

35

could not have been him. What can it possibly mean?"

The only way she could find out was by bringing the speaker of the words to Vidarbha. But how? Then she had a brilliant idea. She would hold another swayamvara. She sent a message to Rituparna informing him, and within hours Rituparna was on his way, driven by his charioteer Vahuka-Nala. Nala was as confused as Damayanti, but at least remembered to take with him the garment that the naga had given him.

As they rode along, questions beat in his mind like the horses' hooves on the road. Why should Damayanti be holding another swayamvara? Had she not understood his message? Did the messengers report that no Nala was at Ayodhya?

Only part of Nala's mind was on the horses; the rest was buried in puzzlement. Faster and faster went the horses. As they drove under a tree the chariot caught a low branch and veered sickeningly towards the edge of the track. There was a terrifying moment as they nearly plunged off, then Vahuka brilliantly brought the chariot back onto the track and steadied the horses.

Rituparna was not angry, only amazed. "What astounding skill!" he said. "We could have been killed. That was a heavy branch of five hundred and seventy leaves."

"How do you know...?" Now Nala was amazed.

"I guessed. Really it is more like counting in a flash. I can tell you how many large stones lie in the road ahead – see, forty-seven – and work out how many will be hit and thrown to one side by our wheels – eleven. That is why I have never been beaten at dice or any other game of prediction."

Nala recalled the naga's prophecy, about exchanging his own skill for Rituparna's. "Teach me about numbers," Nala said, "and in return I will tell you about chariots and horses, then you will do well in the races at the swayamvara."

"Splendid!" said Rituparna, and the rest of the journey was spent teaching each other.

Damayanti was looking out for Rituparna's chariot. When it drew up in the palace grounds she saw no one who looked at all like Nala. She started to despair.

Nala had decided not to reveal himself before he found out why Damayanti had prepared a second swayamvara. So when a servant came to him from Damayanti asking, "Where are you, king and gambler?" he said tantalizingly, "Only Nala knows Nala."

Then he was summoned to Damayanti herself. He could hardly keep from tears at the sight of her. She began asking him questions, looking at him intently, trying to see the young Nala in the old Vahuka.

"Do you know Nala the king? Have you any idea where he is at this moment? Or why he left me?"

With a faltering voice, Nala answered, "What I know is that the demon Kali took over Nala's mind, and filled it with blindness, and made him gamble his whole world away.

"For what reason," Nala went on, "have you now arranged a swayamvara?"

"To bring to Vidarbha the charioteer Vahuka, the speaker of the words that sounded so much like Nala's words." Her lip quivered as she spoke.

Then he stood up before her and with a shout of joy drew on the naga's white cloak. Vahuka, the bent old charioteer, faded into the body and true appearance of Nala. Damayanti wept and wept, and they sat holding each other's hands for a long time.

Pushkara sneered with delight when Nala offered him a last game of dice, this time for their lives. Nala, free of Kali, and knowing the secrets of numbers, toppled Pushkara from his throne and became king again. In his happiness he forgave his brother, and even let him have a small town to rule.

Buddha
and the Swan

One of the enemies of the Buddha was his evil cousin, Devadatta. One morning Siddhartha, with his young pupil, Ananda, was reading in the shade of a favorite tree. He heard the familiar beat of wings overhead and looked up, out over the river. In a moment a group of swans flew into view. They were in formation, and dropped low over the water, flying away from him. He watched them, taking pleasure in their outstretched necks and the graceful, weighty beat of their white wings.

"Why does this give me such joy each morning?" The Buddha spoke his question aloud to Ananda.

"Why do you ask? Isn't it enough that it does?" his pupil said.

"You are right," the Buddha said. He was waiting for the moment when the swans would rise and skim the tops of the trees on the opposite bank.

"Perhaps it is a kind of prayer, watching them…?"

He had no time to think up wiser answers. The flight of one of the swans had suddenly faltered. A wing tipped downward and the bird lost height, coming down with a great splash by the far bank of the river. Siddhartha could see where it was trying to haul itself up the bank, one wing trailing.

Siddhartha knew at once that an arrow had brought it down. He knew whose arrow it was. It could only be Devadatta's. His cousin Devadatta liked hunting swans; the Buddha preferred watching them.

38

"At this moment Devadatta is made a few notches happier by a creature's pain," Siddhartha said. "What's more important, he'll be on his way to find the swan. Let's be there first, Ananda." In a few moments Ananda was rowing the Buddha across the water.

The swan had stayed where it was, in shock. It was wounded. The arrow, with a vicious head of barbed flint, was lodged just above where the left wing emerged from the body. With Ananda holding the flapping bird, Siddhartha knelt and very carefully began to ease the arrowhead back out of the flesh. The bird hissed and struggled, but finally the arrow was out. With Siddhartha clasping the heavy, restless bird in his arms, Ananda rowed them back across the water.

In the shade of the banyan tree, the Buddha washed the bird's wound and then dressed it with some fabric from one of his garments. Then he put the bird down in a natural nest shape between two wiry roots of the tree. Exhausted, it lay quietly, its head stretched forward on the ground.

"Here he comes," Siddhartha said. Devadatta was looking across at them from the other side of the river. He must have seen them take the swan, and now he was coming to claim his prey. The Buddha and Ananda watched the splashing of oars as Devadatta's boat labored across.

"That is my swan!" was the first thing he said as he strode up from the river. "It was my arrow that shot it, and my bow that propelled the arrow. The bird is my prey and my property."

"Was it your river it fell in, too? And your sky it flew in? Devadatta, creatures are not your property because you kill them. They belong to whoever loves them the most and protects them. Your bow and arrow, my swan. I am keeping my swan. Unless you want to shoot me and make me your prey and property as well."

Devadatta shouted. "You're interfering with the natural rights of hunters! I shall take this case to the elders!"

"You're interfering with the natural rights of swans."

Devadatta fumed and stormed, but in the end he gave up and left.

The Buddha looked after the swan till the wing healed. When, after a few weeks, it finally took to the air again, he took special pleasure in seeing it fly with the others again, over the trees and down low across the river. He had re-created the life that Devadatta had almost destroyed.

Shiva Goes Fishing

Of all the gods, Shiva was the greatest yogi, the most powerful meditator. He taught Brahmin priests his own wisdom, which he had learned on the cool Himalayan heights. But his wife, Parvati, often had to listen to his teaching as well…

Shiva could do many amazing things, such as making the stars sway and the earth dance. But one thing he could not do was make his wife Parvati as interested in sacred texts as he was. Once, after spending the day going over one or two sentences in a hymn and explaining the thought behind the words to her, Shiva saw Parvati yawn. The next moment she dozed off completely.

"Parvati, you are not listening! If you cannot follow my simple teaching, you might as well be the wife of a human dolt, with no books and no skill in contemplation. Perhaps you'd prefer to be the wife of a fisherman?"

Why not? Parvati thought. *It sounds nice compared to being told off for going to sleep. Anyway, I can't listen to any more of his mile-long explanations.*

"Parvati?"

When Shiva looked up, Parvati had disappeared. In that moment's pause she had borrowed the body of a small girl on earth, and was walking at the edge of the sea. She came to a village where a few boats were hauled up and some fishermen were mending their nets.

"Hello, child, and where have you come from? And where are you going to?"

Parvati could have said, "I have come from Shiva's heaven, and I am punishing him by doing exactly what he told me to," but it would have sounded strange. Instead she said, "I am lost. My father and mother have been taken away by wicked men. I do not know where to go."

The fishermen stopped their mending. One of them said, "Well, you must be taken in and cared for." Soon there were two or three voices saying, "You can come to our house," and "Stay with us."

The natural kindness of the fishermen touched Parvati. Tears came to her eyes, to think how humans could care for her when Shiva was so cool towards her.

One of the men was a young fisherman whose daughter had been drowned in the floods. He thought how Parvati resembled his own dead child. Other men noticed the same resemblance. Nothing needed to be said; Parvati would go with him.

Parvati found herself taken by the hand and led up the village street. In no time at all she was in her new home and the fisherman's young wife was fussing over her delightedly.

So it was that Parvati, wife of Shiva, became the daughter of a fisherman and his wife. Years passed, and she grew up to be so beautiful that the young men of the village couldn't stop thinking about her. As they gazed down into the deep blue water, searching for the dark shadows of fish, they would imagine her swimming below them. They were at sea, but their thoughts were back at the village.

All those years of human time were only a second or two in the life of Shiva. In the few moments after Parvati had disappeared the god found that he could not concentrate on his yoga and his prayers. Peering down to earth he saw what was happening, and in a jealous rage ordered his servant Nandi to become a great shark and terrorize the village.

The shark Nandi, with Shiva watching from above, followed the boats out to the fishing grounds. When the nets began to fill with fish he tore into them with his steely jaws and shredded them. Then he turned on the boats themselves and attacked them. Day after day the catch was lost and the boats damaged. The men hardly dared to put out to sea. At night, when the mended boats were at their moorings, Nandi would slip into the harbor by the light of Shiva's moon and crunch pieces out of their sides.

The chief of the village called the fishermen to a meeting. "What shall we do?" he said. "If any one of us were rich, he could offer a bag of jewels to any young man willing to risk his life fighting the shark. But we are poor. We have our boats and nets and skill, and that's all."

There was silence.

"I have an idea." It was Parvati's father. "If my daughter agreed..." he said hesitantly, "If she promised to marry the man who caught the shark, perhaps a few would come forward to try. Many of them are in love with her."

The man and his wife asked Parvati whether she could agree to the idea. She did. She had always been grateful to them, and she was very fond of the threatened village and its people.

This was the moment that Shiva had been waiting for. Within an hour of earthly time, a handsome young man was observed strolling along the beach. He joined the men by the boats, who were talking about the best way to catch the shark and marry Parvati.

"I'm from Madura, along the coast. I'm not from here, but can I try to catch the shark?" Shiva asked.

The men looked at each other, wondering which was more important, the village getting rid of the shark, or a villager marrying Parvati. "Yes," one said, "you can try."

As well as Shiva, there were several young men willing to risk their lives. They made their boats ready, loading them with the biggest nets and strongest harpoons they could find.

At dawn on the next day, while the remains of the moon lay on the water, they set out. The air was still cool, the sea quiet.

"There!"

The great fin could be seen in front of them, as the shark patrolled the edge of the fishing grounds.

43

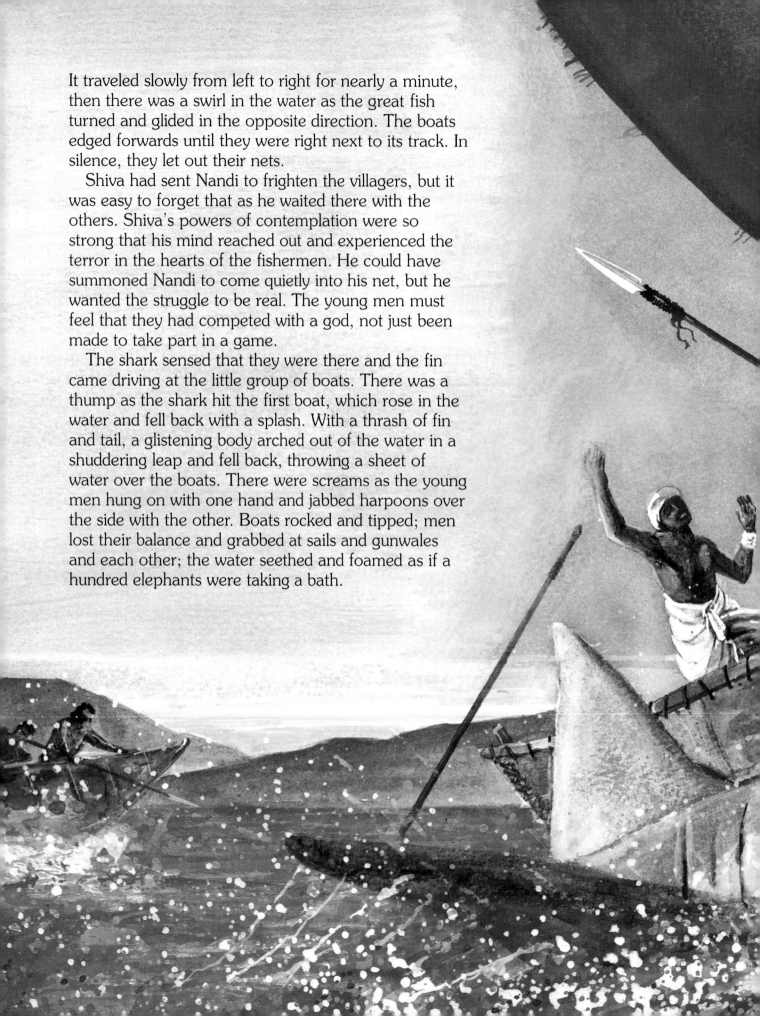

It traveled slowly from left to right for nearly a minute, then there was a swirl in the water as the great fish turned and glided in the opposite direction. The boats edged forwards until they were right next to its track. In silence, they let out their nets.

Shiva had sent Nandi to frighten the villagers, but it was easy to forget that as he waited there with the others. Shiva's powers of contemplation were so strong that his mind reached out and experienced the terror in the hearts of the fishermen. He could have summoned Nandi to come quietly into his net, but he wanted the struggle to be real. The young men must feel that they had competed with a god, not just been made to take part in a game.

The shark sensed that they were there and the fin came driving at the little group of boats. There was a thump as the shark hit the first boat, which rose in the water and fell back with a splash. With a thrash of fin and tail, a glistening body arched out of the water in a shuddering leap and fell back, throwing a sheet of water over the boats. There were screams as the young men hung on with one hand and jabbed harpoons over the side with the other. Boats rocked and tipped; men lost their balance and grabbed at sails and gunwales and each other; the water seethed and foamed as if a hundred elephants were taking a bath.

In all the heaving and thrashing of the water it was hard to make out where the shark was. Then the commotion died down, and the fishermen, looking across at Shiva's boat, saw the fearsome creature flapping quietly in his net. Mysteriously and suddenly, the shark had been overcome. The young men were unharmed, but the stranger had won!

"A miracle! What happened?"

"How did you do it?"

"One second he was in the water," Shiva said, "the next he was in my net."

The fishermen headed for the land, relieved to have caught the shark, but sad as well. The loveliest girl in the village would leave them and fade from their lives.

The next day the god Shiva – the stranger from Madura – was married for a second time, but the first time on earth, to the goddess Parvati – the young adopted girl. The young men watched with sad eyes, but the older people were just happy that the boats could go out again.

After the ceremony, Shiva spoke to the villagers: "I want to give a great blessing to you, father and mother of my wife. To make the blessing greater, I will tell you now that it is the god Shiva who gives it."

And so Shiva told them the whole story. The villagers listened with astonishment on their faces. They were awed to think that their lives had been blessed in such a way, but one or two of the young men felt cheated that a god had come in disguise and taken away the loveliest girl they had ever seen.

As for Parvati, she was pleased to be going back to Kailas, her mountain home. Perhaps she could take more interest in the great books and in Shiva's meditations. She wished she had done that before this small argument with him, which had wasted several moments of their time together.